TROUBLE at TABLE 5

#3:
The Firefly Fix

by **Tom Watson**

illustrated by
Marta Kissi

HARPER
An Imprint of HarperCollins*Publishers*

Dedicated to Jacob (IASPOWYA)

Trouble at Table 5 #3: The Firefly Fix
Text copyright © 2020 by Tom Watson
Illustrations copyright © 2020 by HarperCollins Publishers
Illustrations by Marta Kissi

Library of Congress Control Number: 2020936259
ISBN 978-0-06-295347-6 — ISBN 978-0-06-295346-9 (paperback)

Typography by Torberg Davern
21 22 23 24   PC/LSCC   10 9 8 7 6 5 4 3
❖
First Edition

Table of Contents

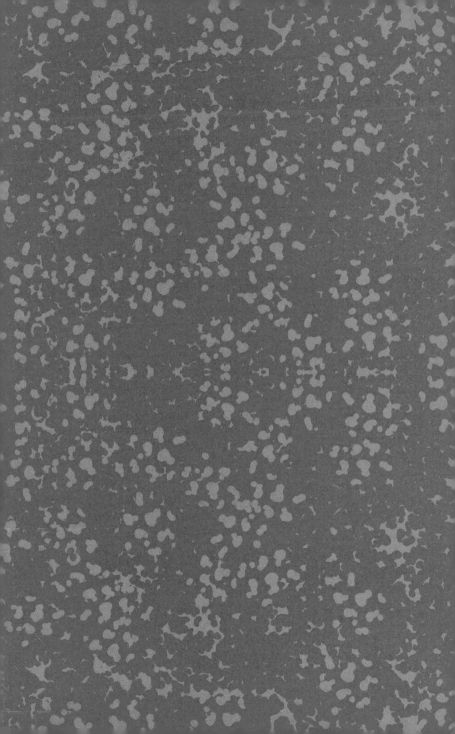

CHAPTER ONE
A STRANGE LIGHT

IT WAS BEDTIME on Tuesday.

But I wasn't in bed.

"Mom! Dad!" I called from the top of the stairs.

"Yes, Molly?" Mom called back.

"There's a strange light outside!" I spoke loud enough to reach all the way to the living room. Mom and Dad like to read down there at night.

"What's strange about it?" Dad said loudly.

"It's like a long, straight beam of light," I answered.

"What color is it?" Mom asked.

"Just white," I said. "It's pretty far away. It's not like blue or red or anything."

"What else is strange?" asked Dad.

"It shoots across the sky every six seconds," I yelled.

"Well, it's an even number, anyway," Mom called. "That's good, right?"

"Right," I called back.

My parents know I like even numbers

way more than odd numbers. Because with odd numbers, there's always something left over. And what are you supposed to do with something that's left over? That just doesn't make sense to me.

Dad called, "We're on the way!"

When they got to my room, Mom, Dad, and I watched the light move across the sky from my window.

"What is it?" I asked.

"Looks like a searchlight," Dad said.

"What's a searchlight?"

"It's a real powerful beam of light," Dad started to explain. "You know the spotlight the school uses for the holiday play every year?"

"The one up in the balcony?" I asked.

"Yes," Dad said and nodded. "A searchlight is like that, only a hundred times—maybe a thousand times—more powerful."

SPOTLIGHT

SIMON AS WORLD'S SKINNIEST SANTA

"How come it moves in a circle like that?" I asked. "How come it goes around once every six seconds?"

"It must be on a rotating platform," Mom answered. She pointed her index finger up in the air and turned it slowly.

"Why is it there?"

"I'm not sure," Dad answered and shrugged his shoulders. "It's kind of an old-fashioned thing, to be honest. I haven't seen one in years. Searchlights are used to attract people."

"Like if there was a traveling circus in town," Mom said, helping out. "They would use a searchlight to get people to come to the circus. The idea was that people would be curious about the light in the sky, follow it, and then have fun at the circus."

"Great example," Dad said.

"A circus would be awesome!" I exclaimed. "Do you think that's what it is?"

"I doubt it," Dad answered. "There aren't too many traveling circuses anymore."

"Bummer," I said. "Then what *is* over there?"

"I don't know," Dad said. He pulled down the window shade while Mom fluffed my pillows. "But it's bedtime now."

But I didn't get into bed. No way.

"Do you really think I can go to sleep without knowing *exactly* where that searchlight is?" I asked. "And *why* it's there?"

It was quiet for two seconds while Mom and Dad looked at each other.

Then Dad laughed.

"All right, Molly," he said. "We'll take you there. Get a hoodie to put over your pj's. It's chilly for a June night. And put on some sneakers."

"Yay!" I yelled and jumped up and down four times. "Thanks, Dad!"

YOU'VE ALREADY READ 534 WORDS. OFF TO A GREAT START!

CHAPTER TWO

IT'S ANNOYING!

WE DIDN'T TALK much as we drove. Dad concentrated on getting us to that searchlight. Mom helped by watching the light and telling him when to turn. I was busy looking out the window. Sometimes when I look out the car window, I'm so busy that I forget to blink. And I have to say in my brain, *"Blink, Molly, blink."*

We got to the searchlight.

It wasn't a cool traveling circus.

It was a boring car dealership.

Dad parked, turned to me, and asked, "How many signs did we pass?"

"Thanks for asking," I said and smiled at him. "We passed thirty-three signs."

"Thirty-three?" Mom asked. "That's an odd number. Do you want to drive around for a minute so you can finish on an even number?"

"No," I said and shook my head. "I want to see the light now."

The searchlight was strapped to the back of a big truck. There was a large red metal box on the ground next to the truck. A bunch of thick rubber cables ran from the red box to the searchlight. We walked closer. The metal box hummed and vibrated.

"What's the big red box for?" I asked.

"I think it's a generator," Dad said. "It runs on gasoline. That searchlight needs a lot of power. If it was just plugged into an outlet, it would probably knock out the electricity in the whole town."

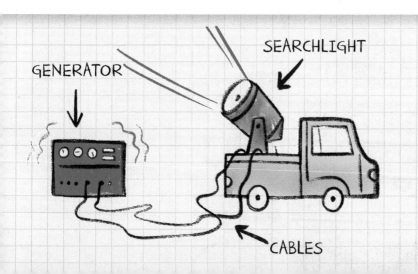

GENERATOR

SEARCHLIGHT

CABLES

"Like during that big storm last year?"

"Exactly," Mom answered.

We stopped about ten feet from the searchlight. The circular motion was calming and rhythmic. I could feel my head rotate on my neck slightly as I watched it turn and turn.

"Why is it here?" I asked. "At a car dealership?"

Dad said quietly, "You're about to find out."

Because I was mesmerized

by that rotating light, I hadn't noticed that a woman had walked up to us.

"I'm Hannah," the woman said. She had a name tag on her shirt. "We've got a big sale going on this week. Great cars. Zero percent financing. Are you interested in upgrading to a new model?"

"No, I'm not," Dad answered politely.

Mom said, "Our daughter saw the searchlight and was curious about it."

Hannah leaned down to look at me. "And what is your name?" she asked.

"Molly Dyson."

"Well, Molly Dyson," Hannah said and smiled, "what do you think of our big light in the sky?"

"I think it's annoying," I said. "I'm awake because I had to find out what it was. And it's Tuesday. It's a school night. My friends Rosie, Simon, and I have to come up with a project tomorrow for the science fair—and make it work by Friday

night. So I should really be sleeping." Hannah seemed a little surprised at my answer. She said, "I'm sorry about that, Molly."

"May I ask you a question?" I said.

"Of course."

"Did you know that you can spell your name backward and forward?"

"I *did* know that," Hannah answered.

"Can I ask you another question?"

"Sure."

"When are you going to turn the light off?"

15

"We're open late this week because of the sale, Molly. We close at ten o'clock," Hannah said. "We'll turn it off a little before then."

"Okay," I said and took Mom's hand. We turned around to go to the car. "Bye."

Dad laughed. Every now and then he laughs a little bit at me. He just thinks I'm funny sometimes.

CHAPTER THREE

STUCK IN MY HEAD

I STOOD AT my window and watched the searchlight make its circular pattern across the sky, flashing by my window every six seconds.

Just like Hannah promised, the searchlight went off right before ten o'clock.

I hadn't realized how much brighter the night was with the searchlight. Now that it was off, I could see how dark it was.

There was no moonlight or starlight—it was cloudy out.

Oh, and there were fireflies. In our backyard. A bunch of them.

How could something so little blink so brightly?

The searchlight needed a big red gasoline-powered generator to shine its light.

Fireflies don't have generators.

The searchlight is used to attract people.

Fireflies use their light to attract other
fireflies. I thought. I didn't know that for
sure.

There was something there.
Right at the edge of my mind.
Something needed to be figured out.
Something needed to be done.

I climbed into bed.

But I didn't fall asleep for
quite a while.

Something was stuck in my head.

Fireflies.

CHAPTER FOUR

THE FIREFLY PROBLEM

I HOPED THAT the fireflies would get unstuck by school the next day. I knew I should really be thinking about the science fair.

But the fireflies didn't get unstuck.

"There's something I have to talk to you guys about," I told Rosie and Simon on the way to lunch. "It's important."

We hustled through the cafeteria line, got our food fast, and sat at a table by ourselves. For lunch that day we had chicken nuggets, a banana, and a scoop of mashed potatoes.

I like bananas because they're the same color on the outside and the inside. The outside is dark yellow and the inside is light yellow. No problem.

I don't like fruits that are one color on the outside but a totally different color on the inside. Like watermelon is green on the outside, but red on the inside. Or apples are red on the outside, but white on the inside.

It just doesn't seem very honest.

You know what I mean?

So I like bananas. I broke mine into eight bite-size pieces.

"Rosie," I said. "Can I ask you something?"

"Here it comes," Simon said.

"What?" I asked. "Here *what* comes?"

"Simon and I could tell something was bugging you," Rosie said. "We just figured it was the science fair. I know you're worried about coming up with a project. We are too."

I smiled. They knew me so well.

Simon asked, "So what is it?"

"It's not the science fair," I answered. "It's fireflies. I want Rosie to tell me everything she knows about them."

"First of all, fireflies aren't flies at all," Rosie began. I knew she'd have good information. She's *so* good at science. That was one reason why we weren't, like, totally panicked about the fair on Friday. We had Rosie on our team.

"They're beetles. When they flash their light, that's called bioluminescence."

I asked, "What else?"

"It's okay to catch fireflies, but you shouldn't keep them for more than a day. And you don't need to poke holes in the jar. Lots of people do that, but you don't have to. You just need to drop something wet in the jar. They like moist air. Their light can be yellow, green, or orange."

I took a banana bite and asked, "Why do they flash their light?"

"To attract a mate," Rosie answered.

"That's what I thought."

"Awesome," Simon said. "I've always wanted to learn about the romantic habits of fireflies."

"Really?" I asked.

"No."

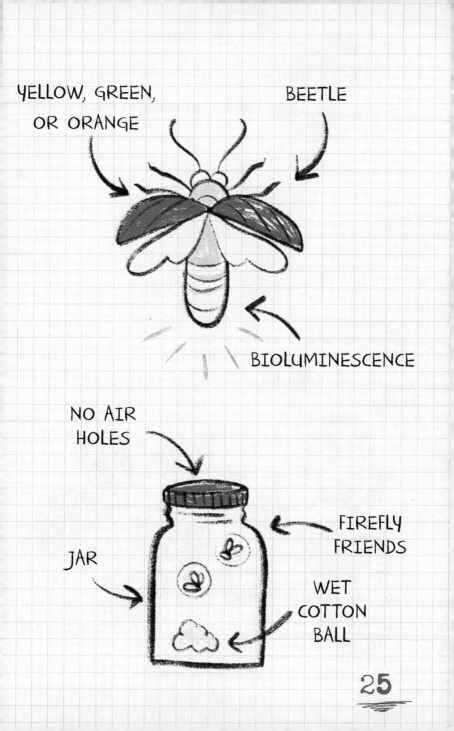

YELLOW, GREEN,
OR ORANGE

BEETLE

BIOLUMINESCENCE

NO AIR
HOLES

FIREFLY
FRIENDS

JAR

WET
COTTON
BALL

25

"Oh," I said and smiled. He was kidding me. "It's not the romance part that's important anyway. It's the attraction part."

Simon and Rosie just stared at me. I needed to explain.

"Last night, Mom, Dad, and I tracked down a searchlight in Bucktown," I said. I pushed my tray to the side. "It was at a car dealership. They use the light to attract customers. After we got home, I watched out my window until they turned it off.

When the searchlight went out, it got really dark. I saw a bunch of fireflies and I started wondering about something. And it got stuck in my head."

"Here it comes," Simon said.

Rosie nodded.

"Searchlights are big and bright and made to attract lots of people," I said and stopped. I leaned toward my best friends. "I want to make firefly light bigger and brighter to attract lots of fireflies."

FOUR CHAPTERS DOWN. YOU MUST BE SUPER FOCUSED!

CHAPTER FIVE

DODGEBALL AND ELECTRIC EELS

GYM CAME RIGHT after lunch. It was a dodgeball day.

You know what dodgeball is, right? It's when two classes run around and throw balls at each other. Mr. Gumposer (we call him Mr. Bulldozer) picked Katie Cunningham and Burt Glass to be captains. They chose the teams. Katie picked Rosie first, which was kind of weird because Rosie isn't very good.

In the first couple of minutes of the game, Rosie, Simon, and I all got hit. We were the first three out. We did it on purpose—we had things to talk about. We sat together near the stacked gym mats by the basketball hoop.

"Okay," I said, looking around at the fifty-seven remaining kids playing dodgeball. "Anybody have any ideas?"

Rosie shook her head, but Simon spoke up quickly.

29

"I came up with something," he said confidently.

"Awesome," I said. "Let's hear it."

"Okay, we need a light that's big and bright to attract lots of fireflies, right?" Simon asked quickly. He talked fast. He had that glazy look in his eyes.

Rosie and I nodded. Ten more kids had been hit in dodgeball.

"Okay, we go to the city zoo," Simon began. "When we get there, we head straight to the electric eel tank in the Sea Life exhibit. When nobody's watching, I'll climb up to the top of the tank. Will you two hold my ankles so I don't fall in?"

We said we would—although I could tell Rosie, like me, was a little worried about where Simon's idea was going.

"Great, thanks," he said and continued.

He spoke even faster. "I'll reach into the tank and grab an electric eel. We'll hurry home and put it in a bucket of water in Molly's backyard. It will light up! Electric eels are real bright, I think. Then all the fireflies in the surrounding area will be like, 'Hey, look at that crazy-big light down there in Molly's yard! Let's go check it out!' There you go. Problem solved."

I looked out at the dodgeball game. Half the kids had been eliminated. We were running out of time.

"Umm, Simon," I said. "It's a great idea and everything, but—"

I didn't say anything else.

Because Rosie interrupted me.

"You can't grab an electric eel!" she yelled. The dodgeball game was loud, so only Simon and I heard her.

"I can't?"

"No!" Rosie exclaimed. "You'll get electrocuted!"

"Oh," Simon said and paused.

Apparently, he hadn't thought of that. "Right. Umm, bad idea."

"Plus, it needs to be firefly light," I reminded him. "It's not just *any* light that fireflies are attracted to. It's *firefly* light."

"Oh, so we need to make their actual light—you know, on their butts or whatever—brighter?" asked Simon. Rosie and I both nodded. "Well, how in the world are we going to do that?"

Rosie answered, "That's what we need to figure out."

But we weren't going to figure it out right then. The first dodgeball game was over—and the second was beginning.

"Come on," Simon said. "It's time to get hit in the head with a ball."

CHAPTER SIX

ROSIE TWIRLS HER HAIR

SCIENCE IS THE last subject on Wednesdays. Simon, Rosie, and I sat at Table 5 while Mr. Willow wrote the science fair schedule on the big whiteboard.

Simon poked me with his elbow and nodded his head toward Rosie. She was twirling her hair. That meant she was trying to figure something out.

"Mr. Willow?" Rosie called from Table 5.

SCIENCE FAIR SCHEDULE

TODAY—CHOOSE A SCIENCE FAIR PROJECT.

THURSDAY—GATHER SUPPLIES AND GET TO WORK.

FRIDAY—FINISH PROJECT.

FRIDAY NIGHT—SCIENCE FAIR!

Before even turning around, he said, "Yes, Rosie?" He knew it was Rosie. Rosie asks lots of questions during science.

Here are some examples of what Rosie has asked Mr. Willow:

"Why is the sky blue?"

"Will time travel ever be possible?"

"Why do we throw salt on sidewalks when it snows?"

This time, Rosie asked, "How does a magnifying glass work?"

Mr. Willow explained that a convex lens bends outward. And two convex lenses put together with both sides bent outward creates magnification. He drew the shape of it on the whiteboard. It sort of looked like a flying saucer.

Mr. Willow asked, "Why do you want to know how a magnifying glass works?"

"Just curious," Rosie answered and glanced at Katie Cunningham at Table 3 real fast. "Can you magnify light? If I shine a flashlight through a magnifying glass, will the light get bigger?"

"Hmm," Mr. Willow said and paused. This was apparently a tough question. "It wouldn't get bigger. The light would actually be more concentrated. Narrower and brighter, like a laser beam."

"Brighter?" Rosie asked. It sounded like she liked that answer.

"Brighter."

"Thank you," Rosie said.

Mr. Willow nodded and began to talk about the science fair some more.

And Rosie started to twirl her hair again. When Mr. Willow finally finished, we were able to talk to Rosie.

"Did you figure out my firefly problem?" I asked, leaning in closer.

"Did you come up with an idea for our science project?" Simon asked.

"Both," Rosie said. "We're going to build something to attract fireflies. It will be our science fair project—*and* it will get the fireflies out of Molly's head."

"That's awesome!" I exclaimed.

Simon gave Rosie a fist bump.

"But there are three problems," Rosie said. You could tell she was excited and nervous at the same time. "Three *huge* problems."

"What are they?" I asked.

"The first problem is Copycat Katie," Rosie whispered and nodded her head at Katie Cunningham. Simon and I knew exactly what Rosie was talking about. Katie had copied Rosie's science fair ideas two years in a row. "We have to keep this idea a secret."

"What's the second problem?" Simon asked.

"I don't know if we can get it done in time," Rosie answered. "We only have two days."

I asked, "And the third problem?"

"I have no idea if it will work."

Then the bell rang.

"Let's go," Simon said, reaching for his backpack on the floor. "We can talk about it on the walk home."

"I can't leave yet," Rosie whispered. She eyeballed Katie again. "I have to ask Mr. Willow one more question—but not until Katie is gone."

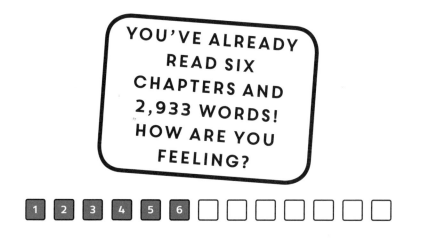

YOU'VE ALREADY READ SIX CHAPTERS AND 2,933 WORDS! HOW ARE YOU FEELING?

CHAPTER SEVEN

SIMON
PICKS A
NAME

WE WALKED TO my house from school and Rosie explained her plan to us. Simon and I thought it might actually work.

"How do we start?" I asked as we got to the back patio.

"We need to get our supplies," Rosie said as she unzipped her backpack and pulled out ten magnifying glasses. "Mr. Willow let me borrow these from the science closet. I told him they were for the science fair."

"Did he ask you what our project is?"

"Yes," Rosie answered and nodded. "But guess who came back into the room to get something from her desk right then?"

"Copycat Katie?" I asked.

Rosie squeezed her lips together, squinted her eyes, and nodded again. Rosie almost never looked mad—but she looked kind of mad right then.

"No way!" Simon exclaimed. "She wants to take your idea? Again?!"

"I didn't want to take the chance, so I told Mr. Willow I wanted it to be a surprise," Rosie said and shook the mad look off her face. She knew we had to get moving. "Let's get what we need."

"We need some big plastic bottles," Rosie said after we'd collected everything else. "Regular water bottles won't work. We need big two-liter soda bottles."

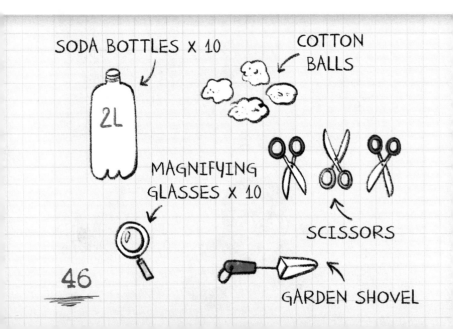

SODA BOTTLES x 10

2L

COTTON BALLS

MAGNIFYING GLASSES x 10

SCISSORS

46

GARDEN SHOVEL

We didn't have any at my house.

But some of my neighbors did.

Simon, Rosie, and I found ten of them in the big blue recycling bins at the end of their driveways. It was kind of weird looking through my neighbors' garbage. But it wasn't gross things—like old food and wet stuff. It was just recycling things—newspapers, plastic bottles, aluminum cans, and cardboard.

We took those ten bottles back to my patio and put them with the other supplies.

"We need an awesome name for our project," Simon said.

Rosie and I thought that was a good idea.

"We're inventing something to attract fireflies," Rosie said. "What's a good name for that?"

"The Great Firefly Catcher?" I suggested.

"It's good, but we're not really catching them," Rosie said. "It's more like we're getting them to meet up in one place."

"I've got it!" Simon exclaimed. "The Fantastic Firefly Fetcher!"

It was perfect. Rosie and I both loved it.

"Okay, we have a name," Rosie said. "Now we have to turn these soda bottles into clear plastic tubes. Oh, and there's something else."

Simon asked, "What's that?"

"We have to figure out one more thing," Rosie said. "And it's going to be tricky."

CHAPTER EIGHT

THE TRICKY THING

WE SAT DOWN criss-cross apple-sauce on the patio to tear the bottle labels off. While we did that, Rosie told us the trickiest part of our project.

"We have to sneak into the greenhouse during school and dig ten small holes with the little shovel," Rosie said.

"We can't go outside during school," I said and bit my lip a little. "It's against the rules. We'll get in big trouble."

"That's why it's the trickiest part," Rosie said.

"We can only go outside at recess," Simon said. "But the greenhouse is locked anyway. Only teachers have keys."

"And the walls and door are made out of glass," I said, picturing the greenhouse. "It's got a screen roof to let rain in—and keep bugs and birds out—but there's no way to get inside."

"It's tricky," Rosie repeated. "But we *have* to find a way in."

GLASS

? ? ?

SCREEN ROOF
LETS RAIN IN,
KEEPS BUGS
AND BIRDS OUT

LOCKED

"I have an idea," Simon said as he scratched his fingernail against a bit of label that was still stuck on his last bottle. "The walls are glass, so we can't get through them. But the top is just a screen. It's pretty loose and flimsy. I think I could get through it."

"How are you going to climb up there?" Rosie asked as we started to cut the tops and bottoms off the bottles to turn them into tubes.

"I'm not going to climb *up*," Simon said. "I'm going to fall *down*."

I asked, "How?"

"I'll jump off the roof of the school, that's how."

"You can't jump off the school roof!" Rosie screamed and laughed.

"Why not?"

"You'll break your legs! Or worse!" Rosie said. Now she was really laughing—like, hard. She was holding her belly.

Simon turned my way for support. He looked at me and said, "I figure the screen roof will slow me down before I smash into the ground."

I shook my head. "It won't slow you down enough. You cannot jump off the school and through the greenhouse roof."

"All right, all right," Simon said, giving up.

It was quiet then. We were each down to our last bottle to cut.

"We can't use the roof by falling through it," Rosie said slowly and twirled her hair, suddenly serious. "But we can use the roof."

"How?" Simon and I asked in unison.

"Tomorrow at recess," Rosie answered. She paused and looked at Simon, then at me. "We're going to play Frisbee."

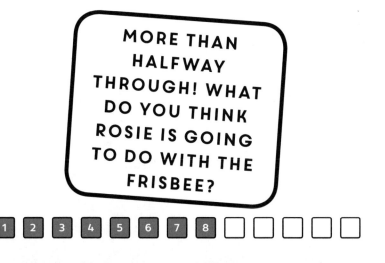

MORE THAN HALFWAY THROUGH! WHAT DO YOU THINK ROSIE IS GOING TO DO WITH THE FRISBEE?

CHAPTER NINE

FRISBEE
TIME

AT RECESS THE next day, Thursday, we launched our plan to get the greenhouse keys.

We hurried toward the back of the playground near the woods. That's where the school garden was. We had figured out our roles at lunch.

I would throw the Frisbee.

Rosie would negotiate with Mr. Willow. Simon would dig the holes.

Rosie and Simon watched Mr. Willow. He was the teacher on the playground with us that day. He was shooting baskets with some of the girls in my class—including Katie.

"He's not looking, Molly," Rosie said. "Go ahead and throw it. Try to get it in the middle of the roof."

I was pretty nervous. I'm not, like, totally athletic or anything. I took a deep breath—and threw the Frisbee.

It was a perfect shot.

Whew.

It landed near the center of the greenhouse's screen roof. We could all see it sag a little in the middle.

"Perfect throw!" Simon exclaimed.

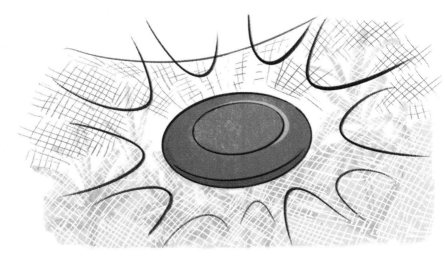

"Okay," Rosie said. "My turn. Let's hope this works."

Simon and I watched as Rosie ran over to Mr. Willow. We couldn't hear her, but we watched as she talked and motioned with her hands. She pretended to throw a Frisbee. She pointed up in the air—and at the greenhouse. She made a poking motion up toward the sky.

And then Mr. Willow did exactly what we wanted him to do. He reached into his pocket, retrieved his keys, and pointed to the one that opened the greenhouse door.

59

Rosie ran back.

"How fast can you dig ten holes?" Rosie asked Simon as she unlocked the glass door to the greenhouse.

"Super fast," he answered and pulled the little shovel from his back pocket.

"Great," Rosie said. She opened the door. "I told Mr. Willow that I was going to poke and nudge the Frisbee with a tomato stake to get it off the roof. I'm going to look busy,

but I'm not actually going to knock it off until you're done."

Simon nodded.

"And Molly," Rosie explained further. "You stand outside and do a lot of pointing and gesturing. Act like you're going to catch it. And spy on Mr. Willow. But don't *look* like you're spying."

"How do I do that?"

Simon said, "Just spy *casually*."

He didn't see the puzzled look on my face. He was already gone.

Rosie went into the greenhouse right after him.

Simon started to dig frantically. And Rosie started poking the Frisbee closer to the edge of the roof so it would

eventually topple over toward me. I could tell she was missing on purpose a lot.

After a few minutes, Simon called, "Five done! Five to go!"

The Frisbee was about three feet from the edge. I glanced over my shoulder as casually as I could. Mr. Willow wasn't shooting baskets anymore. His arms were crossed against his chest. He stared in our direction.

And so did Katie.

"You guys," I called and turned back around. "I think we're running out of time."

CHAPTER TEN

RUNNING OUT OF TIME

"MR. WILLOW IS staring at us!" I scream-whispered.

"Eight!" Simon yelled.

"I can see him!" Rosie scream-whispered back. "He's walking this way. And Katie's with him! She can't find out what we're doing! Hurry, Simon!"

"Nine!"

"He's halfway to us now," Rosie said

urgently—but quietly. She gave the Frisbee a good, accurate nudge and it jumped to the edge of the screen roof. About half of it hung over. "Simon, we have to go! Now!"

"Ten!" he yelled.

I felt Mr. Willow's hand on my shoulder as I stared up at the Frisbee teetering on the edge. Rosie and Simon hustled out of the greenhouse door.

Katie stood next to Mr. Willow. She totally wanted to know what we were doing, I could tell.

"Why did you just yell 'ten!' like that, Simon?" Mr. Willow asked. He didn't sound curious. He sounded like he was accusing Simon of something. It felt like we were in trouble.

I froze. I couldn't move a muscle.

"Uhh," Simon said. He didn't have an answer. I noticed that his hands were in his pockets. He was trying to hide them because they were dirty.

Rosie had an answer though. I knew she didn't like fibbing, but she couldn't give away our science fair project—especially with Katie standing right there.

"He said it would take me at least twelve pokes with the tomato stake to get the Frisbee down," she answered and turned her back toward Mr. Willow to lock the door. I saw her wrist twist as she wiggled the key. She turned back around and continued. "But I won. I got it here in ten."

She handed the keys back to Mr. Willow.

Mr. Willow reached up and grabbed the Frisbee for us.

"Okay, you three," Mr. Willow said as he and Katie headed back toward the basketball hoop. "Move away from the greenhouse if you're going to throw it some more."

We said we would.

When Mr. Willow and Katie and the other girls were shooting baskets again, Simon asked the question that was on my mind too.

"Rosie," he said. "How are we going to

get back in here tomorrow night before the science fair? We'll need the key again."

"No, we won't."

I asked, "Why not?"

Rosie said, "It's not locked."

"But we saw you lock it," Simon said.

"No," Rosie said and smiled. "You— and Mr. Willow—saw me turn my wrist. I never actually put the key in the handle."

Rosie is the best. The absolute best.

CHAPTER ELEVEN

CATCHING TIME

FRIDAY AT SCHOOL, we painted nine Styrofoam balls to look like the planets of our solar system. But that was just our pretend project. Obviously, our real project was about fireflies. We just didn't know if it would work.

So we did a *fake* project at school. We worked on the *actual* project at home.

After dinner, just when it started to get

dark, Simon and Rosie came to my house. We went out to my backyard. We caught as many fireflies as we could.

You can collect a LOT of fireflies in a whole hour.

And we got a ton.

We each had a mason jar with a wet cotton ball inside. That's where we put the fireflies when we caught them. Simon collected the most.

At 7:30, my mom called to us from the back door. It was time to go to the science fair.

Simon, Rosie, and I climbed into the back seat of our car. Their parents were going to meet us at the school.

"What do you have in your backpacks?" my dad asked us from the front seat.

"Just some final supplies for our project," I answered quickly. Simon's backpack was stuffed with most of the clear soda bottle tubes. Mine was jammed with a couple of the tubes and three jars full of fireflies. And Rosie's backpack held the rest of the tubes and all the magnifying glasses.

"You still don't want to tell us what it is?" Mom asked.

"Not really," I said. "It's a surprise."

"Okay," Dad said and smiled at me in the rearview mirror. "No problem."

FIREFLY
JARS ↘

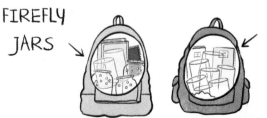

SODA
↙ BOTTLE
TUBES

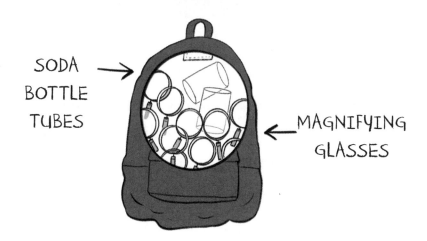

SODA BOTTLE TUBES →

← MAGNIFYING GLASSES

After we parked, Mom and Dad headed toward the school right away.

But we didn't.

"Aren't you guys coming?" Mom asked.

"We have to, umm, go over our presentation one last time," I said.

"Makes sense," responded Dad. "We'll meet you in your classroom."

I nodded. And we waited for them to go inside. We got really lucky then because no other cars pulled into the parking lot.

We sprinted across the playground, heading straight to the greenhouse.

The glass door was unlocked—just as Rosie had left it. And we got to work. There was just enough light for us to see.

A couple of fireflies escaped on the first few holes, but after that we got pretty good at it.

"I don't know, you guys," Rosie said doubtfully when we were done. "I think this might have been a bad idea.

1. I PUT ABOUT TEN FIREFLIES IN EACH HOLE.

2. ROSIE COVERED THE HOLES—AND THE FIREFLIES IN THE HOLES—REAL FAST WITH THE MAGNIFYING GLASSES.

3. SIMON STOOD A CLEAR TUBE ABOVE EACH HOLE.

I don't think it's going to work."

"Maybe we should wait here a few minutes," I suggested. "To see if any fireflies come."

"There's no time!" Simon yelled. "We have to go!"

We raced back to school—and hurried into the classroom.

The science fair was about to start.

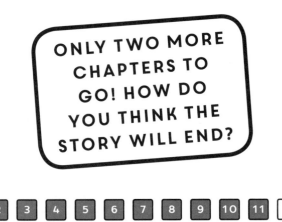

ONLY TWO MORE CHAPTERS TO GO! HOW DO YOU THINK THE STORY WILL END?

CHAPTER TWELVE
TABLE 5'S TURN

OUR PLAN WAS pretty simple.

We had already asked Mr. Willow if we could be last—and he said yes. It was Simon's job to stand near the window and look out at the greenhouse every now and then. If it seemed to be getting brighter or glowing, then we'd know our firefly project had worked. And we could go outside and show it to Mr. Willow.

If it didn't, then we would show our bogus backup solar system project.

Rosie and I were super nervous. We wanted Mr. Willow to go slow to give more fireflies a chance to find the magnified light and be attracted to it.

It took about thirty minutes for Mr. Willow to look at all the other tables. There was a model of a volcano, a Mentos and Diet Coke geyser, a daffodil that had turned blue, and some other cool projects.

Mr. Willow said Katie's solar

TABLE
5

system model was pretty good.

"I knew she'd copy us," Rosie whispered.

I smiled and said, "But she didn't copy the right thing."

We kept looking over at Simon as Mr. Willow got closer and closer to our table.

Simon kept shrugging his shoulders. He came over once to say it was too far away to tell. He thought maybe the greenhouse was glowing a bit—but maybe not. It was so bright in the classroom, it was hard for Simon to see outside.

Mr. Willow was about thirty seconds away from our table. We looked over at Simon one last time.

He shrugged again.

"What should we do?" I whispered to Rosie.

"I don't think we should risk it," Rosie said. I could tell she was disappointed. "If we don't *know* it worked, we better just show our dumb solar system balls."

"It *might* have worked," I whispered.

"We can't risk it," Rosie whispered back.

"It *could* have worked."

"We can't."

"*Maybe* it worked."

"We don't *know*," Rosie whispered and grasped the poster board that covered our Styrofoam planets.

Mr. Willow, our classmates, and all the parents gathered around Table 5.

"Okay, Table 5," Mr. Willow announced. "I'm expecting big things here."

Rosie looked down at the poster board. She knew what was behind it.

I could see the frown on her face. She was embarrassed. She didn't want to lift it up—but Rosie knew she had to.

And then Simon yelled, "Wait!"

CHAPTER THIRTEEN

MR. WILLOW'S DECISION

"**WHAT IS IT,** Simon?" Mr. Willow asked.

"Can we turn the lights off for a few seconds?" Simon asked loudly.

Mr. Willow tilted his head. He was curious. "Sure," he said.

One of the parents flipped the light switch.

Rosie and I snapped our heads to the left and looked outside.

It took a couple of seconds for our eyes to adjust. When they did, we could see the greenhouse.

It was glowing—and blinking.

It wasn't, like, as bright as the sun or anything, but it was definitely glowing.

"It worked!" Rosie whispered to me and squeezed my left hand. I squeezed hers back. And then Rosie pointed toward the window and in a louder voice said, "That's our science fair project!"

Everybody hurried to the classroom windows. It was easy to spot the green-yellow glow in the dark night.

"What is that?" Mr. Willow asked.

"It's our Fantastic Firefly Fetcher!" Simon yelled.

Simon, Rosie, and I led everybody outside to see it. We tried not to run, but we walked super fast across the playground to the greenhouse.

It was covered in fireflies.

Totally.

There were fireflies on all the glass walls, the door, and on the screen roof.

They were everywhere. And there were dozens—maybe hundreds—flying and blinking in the air around the greenhouse too.

Rosie explained how we made the Fantastic Firefly Fetcher to everyone. Simon and I added some details. Simon

was sure to tell everyone that he caught the most fireflies. He was proud of that.

"Is that why you got yourselves into the greenhouse yesterday?" Mr. Willow asked. "Did you throw the Frisbee up onto the roof on purpose?"

Rosie nodded. "We had to dig the holes."

"You know, you didn't have to trick me," Mr. Willow said. "I would have just let you in if you'd told me what you were doing."

"Where's the fun in that?" Simon asked. "Where's the adventure? Where's the pizzazz? Where's the chutzpah?!"

"I don't know what I'm going to do with you three," Mr. Willow said and shook his head. "You're either going to have to stay after school next week for bending the rules . . . or you're going to get first place in the science fair."

He held his hand up under his chin and looked down at the three of us.

We looked up at him. Right then a firefly fluttered down and landed on his index finger. He held it up slowly in front of his eyes. It glowed bright yellow for a couple of seconds.

And then Mr. Willow smiled.

Fun and Games!

THINK

This whole story is about attracting a ton of fireflies. What animal or insect would you want to attract? How could you do it? What would you use? Draw a picture of your plan!

FEEL

Think about how fireflies fly around. They hover sometimes, but they also dip and dart in every direction. Can you move like a firefly? Do it by yourself—how do you feel? Now do it in front of someone else—how do you feel?

ACT

Molly, Rosie, and Simon get most of the supplies for their science project from the recycling bin. What can you make using the stuff that's inside your recycling bin?

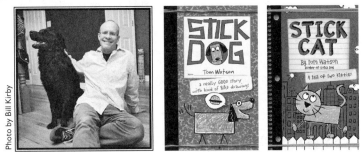

Photo by Bill Kirby

Tom Watson is the author of the popular STICK DOG and STICK CAT series. And now he's the author of this new series, TROUBLE AT TABLE 5. Tom lives in Chicago with his wife and kids and their big dog, Shadow. When he's not at home, Tom's usually out visiting classrooms all over the country. He's met a lot of students who remind him of Molly, Simon, and Rosie. He's learned that kids are smarter than adults. Like, way smarter.

Photo by Krzysztof Wyżyński

Marta Kissi is originally from Warsaw but now lives in London where she loves bringing stories to life. She shares her art studio with her husband, James, and their pet plant, Trevor.